DEVIL'S BRIDGE

Other Avon Camelot Books by
Cynthia DeFelice

WEASEL

Cynthia DeFelice, who is a professional storyteller (part of the Wild Washerwomen team), is also the author of several other books for young people including WEASEL, which is also available from Avon Camelot. She lives in Geneva, New York, with her husband.

DEVIL'S BRIDGE

CYNTHIA DeFELICE

I'd like to thank the people at Larry's Bait and Tackle Shop, Coop's Bait and Tackle Shop, as well as Greg Skomal, wildlife biologist, and my resident fishing expert, Buzz, for providing useful information. I'd also like to thank Helen Manning and Billy Vanderhoop for their friendship over the years, and for all the little ways in which they have helped me know Martha's Vineyard.

While I have used many family names common on the island, all of the characters in this book are entirely fictional. Any resemblance to real people, living or dead, is purely coincidental.

–C.D.

AVON BOOKS
A division of
The Hearst Corporation
1350 Avenue of the Americas
New York, New York 10019

Published by arrangement with Macmillan Publishing Company
Library of Congress Catalog Card Number: 92-7497
ISBN: 0-380-72117-1
RL: 5.0

First Avon Camelot Printing: April 1994

Printed in the U.S.A.

OPM 10 9 8 7 6 5 4 3 2

For Chip and Hank and all the good times fishing

AUTHOR'S NOTE

The rocky ledge known as Devil's Bridge, on Martha's Vineyard in Massachusetts, stretches out from the clay cliffs at the island's northwest tip. There, in the town of Gay Head, you will also find the headquarters of the Wampanoag Indians, whose ancestors lived on that part of the island long before white people came.

For forty-two years the island has held an annual month-long fishing derby. Striped bass were the focus of the contest for many years. Then the stripers began to disappear. As their number decreased, laws were passed to protect them from overfishing and they were excluded from the contest. Now derby entrants try for bluefish, bonito, and false albacore instead. As of this writing, stripers are making a tentative comeback, but they are still not among the species included in the contest. Perhaps someday, with continued restraint on the part of sport and commercial fishermen, and adherence to regulations limiting pollution in the areas where bass live and spawn, large numbers of stripers will once again roam the seas along the east coast. Meanwhile, protection of habitat, and "catch and release fishing," as practiced by this novel's characters Ben Daggett and his friend Jeff Manning, represent the best hope for stripers and many other species of fish.

DEVIL'S BRIDGE

CHAPTER 1

Pop and I walked quickly down the beach to our favorite fishing spot, the shallow, rocky waters known as Devil's Bridge. I was almost running, I was so eager to start casting. Tossing my bucket onto the sand, I headed for the water's edge with my rod.

"Hold it, Ben," Pop called, laughing. "You'll need this, I think." He held out a medium-sized blue popper, our lucky lure, the same kind of lure Pop had used to catch the largest striped bass ever taken from the waters around Martha's Vineyard, the island where we lived.

I looked at my rod. "Yeah, that would help, I guess," I said, grinning back at Pop. I tied the cigar-shaped plug onto my line with a careful knot.

Pop and I stood looking out to sea, the foamy tips of the waves almost reaching our shoes. We were watching for what Pop called "shaky water." That was water that looked different because a big fish was feeding right below the surface. We were hoping to see the telltale shape of a fin or get a quick glimpse of a fish's body. We watched for the sudden, panicked appearance of a cloud of bait jumping from the water to escape being eaten. At the same time, we were listening for the popping sound a striper made as it fed near the surface of the water and the excited screeching of terns and gulls as they dipped over schools of feeding fish.

"The tide'll be changing soon," I told Pop.

"And it's just about sunset," he answered with a smile.

"Perfect," I said.

"Yep," Pop agreed. "Fishing ought to be real good in about an hour."

"Are you going to wait?" I asked.

"I think so," said Pop. "I'll gather some wood so we can have a fire later. You go ahead and fish if you want."

"No," I said. "I'll wait, too."

After we'd gathered a pile of driftwood, we sat on the sand and watched the sun sink closer and closer to the ocean.

"Tell me about when you caught the big fish," I said.

"You don't want to hear that old story, do you?" asked Pop, still gazing out to sea.

"Yes," I answered truthfully. A lot of the guys down

at Squid Row—that was the bait shop and gas dock where all the fishermen hung out—had told me about Pop's big fish, but Pop had never talked about it himself.

"It was a long time ago . . . sixteen and a half years," said Pop.

"Five years before I was born," I figured aloud. "Well, five and a half."

Pop poked at the sand with a piece of wood. "That fish was probably twenty-five years old when I caught it," he said. "Probably a great-granddaddy."

"And fifty-eight inches long, weighing sixty-six pounds, seven ounces," I recited proudly. "The island's record striper, caught by Captain Jack Daggett right here off the shore at Devil's Bridge."

"Well, there you go," said Pop with a laugh. "You know the whole story already."

"No, Pop," I said. "You never told me what it was like. I mean, how did it feel to catch a fish that big? Did you know it was a record?"

Pop nodded. "I was pretty sure of it. Up until then, the island record was fifty-something pounds, and the fish I caught looked a lot bigger than that to me." Pop stopped. He was quiet for what seemed like a very long time.

I was about to ask Pop what had happened next when he said, "You asked how I felt. I was excited, there's no doubt about that. I'd never seen such a big bass. I remember looking at it—it seemed so huge—and it was very silvery-looking in the moonlight. And I remember feeling lucky to have caught such a beautiful fish, lucky even to have *seen* it. And later, after it was dead and I found out I'd set a record, everybody made a big fuss about it. But I kept thinking about how beautiful that fish had looked swimming in the moonlight, and the idea came to me that fish don't care anything about the record books."

Pop's face was lit with an orange glow from the setting sun. I looked at him, confused. "Weren't you happy?"

"Oh, I was, I guess," he said. "But I didn't feel as happy as I thought I would."

I didn't get it. "But, Pop," I said, "You're a fisherman. You kill fish every day."

"I know, Ben. And there's no better way for a man to make a living, don't misunderstand me. I take fish that are needed for food, and I'm proud to do it. But stripers are game fish, and there was something, well, something *majestic* about that big fish; that's the only word I can think of.

"Right now," Pop went on, "it would make me happy to think that there was a big striper out there"—he pointed to the sea—"just swimming free and spawning and growing old."

"Well, I don't know about you," I said, getting up and reaching for my rod, "but I'm going to find out!"

I pulled on my waders, picked up my rod, and headed for the water. I brought the rod back over my shoulder, ready to cast and—

"Ben!" It was my mother's voice, calling up the stairs, jarring me out of my dream. I opened my eyes.

"Ben, honey? Time to get up. The bus will be here in half an hour."

I sat up in bed and the real world came crashing over me like a wave of cold, salty water. I wasn't fishing with Pop. The day I'd been dreaming about had happened over a year ago. I was in my room. I had to get up and go to school. When I went downstairs, Pop wouldn't be sitting at his place at the breakfast table, listening to the marine weather forecast. Pop was dead. He wouldn't ever be going fishing again.

CHAPTER 2

That afternoon, after school, my friend Jeff Manning and I checked the gear we had hidden in our secret cave in the clay cliffs: two sturdy surf-casting rods, the red bucket with fishing lures hanging by their hooks around the rim, my dad's old lantern, and, in the far corner, our sleeping bags, warm jackets, and rain gear.

"Do you think we should have an extra rod?" I asked anxiously.

"If we catch a striper big enough to break one of these rods, we'll stop fishing and run to contest headquarters to enter it," Jeff answered, grinning. "We won't need another rod."

"I guess not," I replied quickly, anxious to change the subject. Didn't Jeff know it was bad luck to talk too much about catching a prize-winning fish? Better to concentrate on being prepared: Study the tides and the wind, check your knots, sharpen your hooks, keep your eyes and ears open. That's what Pop always said. Then you'd be ready if the big fish came along.

"I guess we're all set," Jeff said.

"Yeah."

The wind was blowing from the northwest, which meant it was sweeping right in off the ocean, and the damp, salty spray whipped through the narrow entrance to the cave and right through the T-shirt I'd worn to school that morning. I was cold and hungry. I looked at my watch. Uh-oh. I was already late for dinner.

"Let's go," I said. "I'm five minutes late. Mom's probably called the cops."

We squeezed through the cave's entrance, walked down the steep face of the cliff, and headed along the beach to where we'd left our bikes. When we reached the narrow path through the dunes, we walked carefully to avoid the poison ivy that grew like crazy all over the island. Now that it was the end of October, the poison ivy had turned a deep, reddish orange that seemed to warn, Keep away! But during the summer it was an innocent-looking green, and I couldn't help feeling a little sorry for the tourists who tramped right through it every year on their way to the beach.

"I'll meet you after school tomorrow," said Jeff, jumping onto his bike.

"Okay."

"We'll go right to my house, make some sandwiches and stuff, and we'll be fishing by four o'clock!" Jeff said excitedly. Then he asked, "What are you going to tell your mother?"

It was a good question. The islandwide Striped Bass Derby began the following day, Friday, at six o'clock in the morning and lasted the entire weekend, ending at six o'clock Sunday evening. Jeff and I had to go to school, but we planned to bike to the beach as soon as possible, get our gear, and start fishing at the rocky point below the cave. We were going to fish all night, and every other minute of the weekend that we could.

The only trouble was my mother. I was lucky she'd let me enter the derby at all, but she had absolutely forbidden me to fish at night. I'd reminded her of what she knew very well, that the best time for fishing for big stripers was at night, in the dark, but I might as well have been talking to the stone jetty down at the harbor. "You'll be home by dark or you won't go fishing at all," she'd said. Here I was, almost thirteen, for cripe's sake, and she treated me like I was two.

"I was thinking about saying I'll be spending the night with you," I answered.

"Well, you will be," said Jeff with a grin. "Except we're going to be spending it at the beach, fishing."

I tried to smile back. "Yeah, but you know what she'll think—that I'm sleeping over at your house."

Jeff whistled. "It's kind of risky," he said. "She might call my mom. And won't she figure I'll be fishing?"

"Probably, but I can't think of anything else. Can you?"

Just then we saw a blue pickup coming down the road, Jeff's father at the wheel. He pulled up alongside us. "You boys planning your winning strategy?" he asked.

"We sure are, Mr. Manning," I said.

"What's it going to be? You fishing from shore or coming out with Betty and me in the *Squeteague*?"

"We're going to try Devil's Bridge, Dad," said Jeff.

Mr. Manning nodded. "Good spot. Going to break your old man's record this year, is that it, Ben?" he asked. "I'd sure like to think there's a fish out there that's sixty-six pounds, I can tell you that. And if there is, I'd like to see Jack Daggett's son be the one to catch it."

"Me, too," I said.

"Well, Betty and I'll be taking the boat and heading out off Noman's Island. You boys are welcome to come along."

"Thanks, Mr. Manning," I said.

"I guess we'll stick to our plan, Dad," said Jeff. "But maybe we'll come out in the boat on Saturday," he said, looking at me questioningly.

I shrugged. "Maybe," I said. If Jeff wanted to go out in the boat with his parents, that was fine with me, but I didn't think I'd go. I had decided I was fishing in the same place and in the same way Pop had always fished for stripers, and that meant fishing off the shore, casting into the rocky waters of Devil's Bridge.

Jeff told his father he'd be right home, and Mr.

Manning turned onto the Lobsterville Beach road. Jeff said, "So you tell your mom you're coming to my house tomorrow night. What about Saturday?"

"I don't know," I answered miserably. "I'll worry about that later, I guess."

"Yeah. Well, I'll see you tomorrow," called Jeff, following his father home.

I went the other way, pedaling hard against the wind, which seemed to be getting stronger all the time. Good, I thought, this wind will get the water churning. Stripers liked it when the waves stirred up the bait fish.

I was breathing hard by the time I reached my driveway. A shiny silver Cadillac was parked by the back door. "Oh, brother," I muttered. "Barry the Bozo's here. Just what I need."

I walked into the dining room, where Mom was already sitting at the dinner table. With her, in my father's chair, was Barry Lester.

Mom let out a sigh of relief when she saw me. "Thank goodness you're safe," she said.

"Mom, I'm only a couple minutes late."

"That's long enough for me to imagine all sorts of terrible things, Benjamin Daggett. Where have you been?"

"At the beach," I mumbled, slipping into my chair.

"The beach?" she asked. "What were you doing at the beach?"

"Nothing," I said. "Just messing around with Jeff.

We lost track of the time. I'm okay. Nothing happened to me. What could happen to me at the beach?"

My mother's face got a funny, crumply look, and, too late, I realized what I'd said.

Pop had died last September, during Hurricane Lois. He had been offshore fishing for tuna when the storm came up too suddenly for him to get in. Bits of his boat, and later his body, had washed up on the shore of Cuttyhunk Island.

Mom hadn't been near any beach since. She hadn't set foot down at the docks, hadn't gone near the water in a whole year. When Pop was alive, Mom went fishing with him all the time. When I was born, she just took me along. Pop used to say proudly that I'd been raised on salt spray, diesel fuel, and bilge water. Mom had helped Pop run the outriggers and put out the nets, rig the rods for tuna and mackerel, rake for scallops, and set and pull lobster pots, and soon I was helping, too. But the hurricane had changed all that.

Hurricane Lois. Just remembering that name made me feel mad and stunned, the way I'd felt when I heard what had happened to Pop. How could a storm with a sweet, stupid name like Lois take my father away?

Now all Mom did was worry that something was going to happen to me, and it was driving me nuts. She was especially nervous these days because fall was hurricane season. If she had her way, I'd probably never go out of the house except to go to school, and I'd never, never go near the ocean. Which was ridiculous if you lived on an island like Martha's Vineyard and if, like me, you planned to be a fisherman.

There was an awkward silence after my dumb question about the beach. Then, in a bright, fake-sounding voice, Mom asked, "Aren't you going to say hello to Mr. Lester, Ben?"

Keeping my eyes on my plate, I muttered, "Hi."

"That's enough of this 'Mr. Lester' business, Kate," said Barry the Bozo in the same kind of too-jolly voice my mother was using. "I'd like Ben to call me Barry. No need to be so formal. We're all friends here," he went on, tilting back in Pop's chair and rubbing his hands across his stomach, which hung loosely over his belt. "Your mother tells me you've entered the derby, Ben."

It wasn't a question, really, so I didn't answer. I just kept shoveling food into my mouth fast so that I could leave the table.

After another awkward silence, my mother finally said, "Ben?" There was a warning in her voice.

"Yeah," I said, still without looking at Barry. "Mom, could you pass the milk, please?"

Mom handed me the milk with a pleading look. I knew she wanted me to make nice, polite conversation with Barry Lester. Didn't she see how wrong he looked, sitting there in Pop's chair, his soft, chubby white hands clasped over his stomach? For a second I saw Pop's hands, strong and brown and callused from a life spent at sea. Fishing was the best kind of work there was, Pop always said. Out fishing, a man could be free. Barry Lester sat in an office, renting cars to tourists, filling out papers with his soft, white hands. How could Mom expect me to have anything to say to a man with hands like that?

"What kind of fish is it you're after?" asked Barry.

The contest was called the Striped Bass Derby. What did he think I was after, goldfish?

"Stripers," I answered.

"I expect you'll need some bait," he said. "Perhaps after dinner we could go out and dig some earthworms." He looked proudly at my mother, as if he'd just said something brilliant.

Worms! Didn't this guy know anything?

Mom jumped in quickly, saying, "Earthworms really work better in fresh water, Barry. If you fish for stripers with bait, you usually use big eels. But Ben plans to fish with plugs, I think. Isn't that right, Ben?"

I nodded.

"Plugs?" asked Barry, looking confused.

"Lures," explained Mom. "They're made of metal or plastic. When you reel them in, they look like a bait fish swimming through the water. Ben," she said, turning to me, "show Barry some of your bass lures."

All my lures were in the cave, ready for the next night's fishing, but I couldn't tell Mom that. I had to change the subject fast.

"My father was a great fisherman," I blurted.

"Oh?" said Barry faintly.

All of a sudden I found myself talking a mile a minute. "He holds the island record for striped bass. Everybody from around here knows about it."

Barry Lester had probably never been in Chick's Tackle Shop, which served as headquarters during the fishing derby, so I told him about the record board on the front wall of the store and how Pop's name was carved right on the top. "Nobody else around here has come close to catching a fish that big," I finished proudly.

There. That should let Barry Lester know that sitting in Pop's chair didn't mean he was even close to taking Pop's place. That ought to show Mom that even though she had forgotten Pop, I hadn't.

"But you're going to beat the record this weekend, is that right?" asked Barry, smiling at me eagerly.

Right then, with Barry Lester grinning at me like a jack-o'-lantern, I wasn't sure what to say. My father's name had been up on that board since before I was born. Putting my name up there would be sort of like . . . like Barry sitting in Pop's chair.

I shrugged, wishing I'd just kept my mouth shut. "I'd better get started on my homework," I mumbled. I got up from the table and began stacking plates.

Mom said, "Barry would like to take us out to dinner tomorrow night, Ben."

"Mom, I'll be *fishing*."

"Well, I thought that maybe afterward—"

"I meant to ask you," I said, interrupting, "Jeff wondered if I could spend the night. That way I'll be able to go out in the boat with him and his parents early Saturday morning."

I kept my head down as I scraped the plates so that I didn't have to look at her face. It was the first big lie I had ever told her, and I felt bad about it. But it was her own fault, I reasoned. If she'd stop worrying so much and let me do things like other kids, I wouldn't have to lie.

"Oh," Mom said quietly. "I guess that will be all right. I'll give Jeff's mother a call to make sure she doesn't mind."

"You don't have to," I said quickly. "It's okay. I saw Mr. Manning this afternoon."

Another lie. Well, not really. I *had* seen Jeff's father. But of course he hadn't said a word about my sleeping over. Feeling desperate to escape, I hurried to the kitchen with the stack of dishes, went straight to my room, and closed the door.

CHAPTER 3

Lying on my bed, I stared at the cracks in the old plaster ceiling. When I was a little kid, I saw things in the cracks: a ship, an old man's face, a lighthouse, a rabbit. But now I stared without seeing anything, my mind spinning like a radar scanner on the cabin of a boat.

Ever since I could remember, people on the island had talked about Pop and his record striped bass. They were always saying things like, "Of course, there'll never be another fish like the one Jack Daggett caught," or, "No one knows how to catch 'em like Cap'n Daggett."

Once, when I was four years old, Pop had taken me with him to Chick's. Chick had pointed to the record board and said, "That fish your daddy caught was twice as big as you, young fellow. Why, a small fry like you would be just a snack for a fish like that one." Ever since that day, that fish had been swimming in my imagination: huge and silvery green, with dark stripes along its sides, the biggest striped bass ever seen on the island, the fish that only my father could have caught.

Every time Everett Larsen, down at the fish market, saw me he said, "Soon you'll be bringing me fish like your father used to, won't you, Ben?" Charlie, the captain of the *Maggie May*, once said, "You've got fishing in your blood, Ben. The Daggetts have always been fishermen." I couldn't remember a time when I hadn't been introduced as Jack Daggett's son, or "son of the best fisherman around these waters," or "son of the man who holds the record for striped bass."

That afternoon Mr. Manning had asked me if I was going to break my father's record, and now Barry Lester had said the same thing. It seemed that it was something folks expected of me.

It was what I wanted to do. It was what Pop would have wanted, what he'd have been proud of. Wasn't it?

I thought about what Pop had said about the record. He'd been happy and excited, he'd said, but there had been something else. . . . I didn't really understand it.

I did know that when stripers started to become scarce in our waters and everywhere else, lots of fishermen were angry, and there were arguments all the time down at Squid Row. Some said the government ought to keep their noses out of it, and let a fisherman make an honest living.

Others said that if someone didn't do something about pollution and overfishing, there wouldn't be any fish left to catch.

My father had been in favor of the regulations, even though some of his friends didn't agree. He'd said the fishery was fragile, and fishermen had a responsibility to protect it. He'd said it was plain common sense to care for the thing that provided his own livelihood.

The regulations changed according to the bass population. Some years no bass at all could be taken. Other years there were limits on the size and number of fish a person could keep. I knew that some people broke the rules and kept illegal bass. But not Pop. I remembered his saying something about leaving some fish for me and my kids to catch.

For about ten years, the Striped Bass Derby had become the Bluefish Derby. Now stripers seemed to be coming back, the regulations had loosened up, and the island was once again holding a Striped Bass Derby, only with new rules. Now you were supposed to kill and enter a striper only if it was really big—fifty inches or longer. That way lots of little fish wouldn't be killed. If no one caught a big striper, the prize money went to the biggest bluefish, bonito, or false albacore. And if someone caught a fish bigger than my father's and set a new record, the five-thousand-dollar prize money doubled.

People were excited and optimistic, too. After all the years with no fishing for stripers, they figured there just *had* to be some really big fish out there. There had to be.

If I caught one and won the derby, Mom would have to see that I wasn't a kid anymore. And if I caught a really big one and broke Pop's record, she'd have to understand that I was a fisherman like Pop, and just as good.

Not to mention that we could really use ten thousand dollars. Mom had a good job at the town hall, but I knew she worried about money. If I won, I could help out. Maybe I could even buy a skiff and outboard motor. I'd already picked out the one I wanted: a fourteen-foot aluminum runabout with a twenty-five horsepower motor. It was perfect—quick and easy to handle and to pull up on the shore, and gas wouldn't cost too much. With a boat, I'd be able to go anywhere. With a boat, I could be a real fisherman. With a boat, I could roam the seas like a fish. Like Pop had. With a boat, I'd be free.

CHAPTER 4

At school the next day, no one learned very much, at least not about school subjects. Most of the boys and a lot of the girls were entered in the derby, and if *they* weren't, their parents or uncles or neighbors were. A lot of the teachers were fishing, too, so talk ran more to tides and lures and "hot spots" than to past participles, the colonial period, or metric measurement.

Mrs. Madison, my English teacher, asked me where I was going to fish, and we spent most of fifth period talking about how Devil's Bridge had gotten its name. It wasn't really a bridge, of course, but a group of rocks that barely showed above the water at high tide. Mrs. Madison said so many ships had been wrecked on those rocks that the sailors used to say the devil himself had put them there. Meg Taylor said that was silly; everyone knew that the rocks had been dumped there by a glacier.

Jeff raised his hand and said, "The Wampanoags have a story about it, too." The Wampanoags were the natives who had lived at the end of the island before white people came. Jeff and a couple other kids in the class were descended from them. "The legend is," Jeff went on, "that there was a giant named Moshup who lived in a cave in the clay cliffs. He brought the rocks to build himself a bridge to the mainland. But one day while he was working, a big crab bit his toe, and he quit halfway through the job."

The bell rang and I said to Jeff, "Well, all I know is that those rocks make the greatest striper fishing spot on the whole island. Only two more periods and we'll be there!"

As soon as the bus dropped us off, Jeff and I ran to his house, where Mrs. Manning was already making tuna fish and peanut butter and jelly sandwiches.

"Thanks, Mom," said Jeff. "You didn't have to do that. We were going to make our own."

"I know," said his mother, putting the top layer of bread on the six sandwiches lined up on the counter. "But I knew you were anxious to get out there and catch the big one. There. What else are you going to take?"

Jeff reached into the cupboard, grabbed a big bag of

corn chips and two packs of cookies, and took a six-pack of soda from the refrigerator.

"Here," said Jeff's mother, "take this along, too. It's hot cocoa. It's going to be pretty chilly out there tonight." She handed Jeff a thermos and added, "Do you two have some warm clothes with you?"

We nodded, putting the food into our backpacks. We were ready.

"You boys be careful now," Mrs. Manning called from the doorway as we rode down the driveway on our bikes. "And good luck!"

"You, too!" we shouted.

Finally we had the whole weekend ahead, with nothing to do but fish! I couldn't stop smiling, even though the cold wind made my teeth hurt.

Jeff and I zoomed down the beach road, hid our bikes, and walked across the damp sand to the cliffs. Leaving the packs on the beach, we climbed the steep, craggy mounds of red, black, white, and yellow clay. Their colors were dazzling in the afternoon sunlight, and I had to squint to see the narrow entrance to our secret cave. Inside, when our eyes had adjusted to the darkness, we found our gear just the way we had left it.

Jeff and I had discovered the cave three years earlier and had vowed not to tell anyone about it, but I had slipped one night and mentioned it to my father. To my surprise, not only did he know about the cave, but it had been his secret hideout when he was a boy. He'd even carved his initials on the back wall, where I found them later.

I didn't know why, but since Pop died, the cave was the place where I felt closest to him, and when I missed him so bad I didn't know what to do, I went to the cave. Sitting in its damp coolness, looking out at the sea, I could pretend he was with me; I could hear his voice, almost feel his hand on my shoulder.

"What lure are you going to start with?" Jeff asked, picking up his rod and tackle box.

I didn't have to think about that. "A blue popper," I answered.

"Mr. Olsen says they're hitting on yellow," Jeff said doubtfully. Mr. Olsen was our math teacher.

"Mr. Olsen can fish with yellow, then," I replied. "I'm using blue."

"I think I'll try metal," Jeff said as we descended the cliffs. "Or maybe a bucktail," he added.

I laughed. "We've got all night," I said. "You can try 'em all!"

"Yeah!" shouted Jeff, beginning to run.

"We can fish our brains out!" I called.

"You already did that a long time ago, Daggett," said Jeff with a wicked smile.

"Maybe I did," I said, tying the popper onto my line. "But when I'm hauling 'em in and you're begging to use one of my lures, we'll see if you think I'm so dumb."

I stepped into the waders that used to belong to my mother. They were like big rubber overalls with boots attached. I loved the feel of them. With waders on, I wasn't stuck on land anymore. I was almost a creature of the sea. I could walk out into the crashing surf up to my waist, with the cold water swirling all around me, and be warm and dry inside.

Holding my rod straight back over my shoulder, I brought it forward with a smooth, forceful motion that sent my plug flying far out into the breaking waves. I aimed just to the left of a large rock, waited a minute to let the lure land, then began reeling it in slowly, holding the rod tip high so that the lure skimmed across the surface, creating a disturbance that the stripers would, I hoped, mistake for a wounded, struggling bait fish.

It was a good cast. Reeling carefully to avoid another, smaller, rock and a floating clump of seaweed, I brought the plug in to shore and prepared to cast again. Jeff was fifty yards or so down the beach, flinging a metal spoon into the water. I didn't have to see his face to know that it was a mask of concentration. There are some things, like washing the dishes, or riding a bike, or mowing the lawn, that you can do while you're thinking about something else. But not fishing, and especially not fishing during a derby, when so much is at stake.

I felt the steady tug on my lure as I brought it through the water, ready to set the hook if a fish struck. The salt spray filled my eyes and nose, the sun sank lower in the sky and sparkled on the water, and I felt the kind of happiness I felt only when I was fishing.

"I got one!" I heard Jeff's excited shout and looked over to see his rod bowed over from the pull of a fish. The next moment I, too, felt a sudden strike, and my reel screamed as the fish took out line.

"I got one, too!" I hollered. "It's acting like a blue—"

All at once—nothing.

I was right. It had been a bluefish. Its sharp teeth had cut right through my line. "It got my lure," I called disgustedly. "Darn pests," I muttered as I reeled in my empty line. I didn't mean it, though. Bluefish were strong fighters, good to eat and fun to catch, but when you fished for them you used a piece of wire between your lure and your line so that they couldn't bite their way free. The trouble was, other fish, like stripers, were more picky, and when they saw the wire, they wouldn't bite.

Jeff was lucky; he hauled in a small blue without losing his lure. I walked over and watched him carefully unhook the fish, hold it in the water, move it forward and back a few times to get oxygen passing through its gills, and release it. Maybe a bluefish would end up winning the derby, but there was no reason to keep a small one like that.

"I'm going to wait until these little blues pass through," I said. "I don't want to lose another lure."

"I think I'll keep casting in case that fish has got a big brother," said Jeff.

"Okay. I guess I'll go check out the action on the other side of the point."

CHAPTER 5

Grabbing a sandwich from the pack, I headed up the beach. The island came to a point at its farthest northwest tip, and as I rounded the curve of the beach I lost sight of Jeff. The cliffs had eroded over the years, sending huge boulders that were trapped in the clay tumbling to the beach below. I was walking among them in the shallow water, looking for signs of fish, when I thought I heard voices over the roar of the waves. Looking ahead, I saw two figures standing close together by a large rock. The wind was blowing toward me, carrying the sounds of their voices. I squinted, trying to make out who it was, and caught a snatch of their conversation.

". . . was thinking I'd have it mounted, put it on the wall, show everybody—"

"Mounted? Are you crazy? After that fish gets weighed, you get rid of it, hear me? Get rid of it!"

"Seems a shame—"

"Listen to me. It'll be a bigger shame if we get caught, you fool. Now forget about it."

For a minute there was silence. Then, "Are you sure I should enter it on the first day? It might look suspicious."

"We're lucky to have kept it alive this long."

"Six days isn't so long."

"No sense pushing our luck."

"What if the judges find the mercury?"

"How're they going to do that?"

My heart was as loud as the waves that pounded the shore, and I strained to listen.

"What if they gut it?"

"Would you just relax? That's the beauty of it. Even if they gut it, they won't find the mercury. They're going to weigh it, they're going to see that it's a record fish, and they're going to give us a lot of money. Listen, there's no way to tell. And the fish ain't gonna be talking, you see? We divvy up the money, I go my merry way, you get to be a big hero here on the island. End of story. Happily ever after, the whole bit. That's if you don't blow it."

I couldn't believe what I was hearing. They were talking about cheating in the derby! The wind shifted, and I couldn't hear the smaller man's reply. Leaning closer, I lost my balance and fell forward slightly. The sudden movement caught the eye of the larger man, and he looked my way. There was silence. It even seemed that the waves had stopped crashing.

"Hey, you, kid!" he called.

"Yeah?" I answered casually, stepping away from the rock as if I hadn't been hiding, but merely walking along.

"What are you doing?" he asked. His eyes narrowed, a scowl twisted the corners of his mouth, and smoke from a cigarette snaked slowly from his nostrils.

Now that I could see both men clearly, I recognized the smaller one from the docks. It was Freddy Cobb, who fished with Captain Norton on the *Aquinnah*, looking like a scared rabbit. I didn't recognize Freddy's companion, but I sure didn't like the way he was looking at me. I knew better than to let on that I had heard anything.

"Hi, Freddy," I said, trying to sound normal. Freddy gave me a short nod. To the big man I said, "What do you think I'm doing? Fishing."

"How long you been standing there?" he asked.

"I just came around the point," I said. "We got into some small blues so I came to see if there was anything happening here."

"No," answered Freddy quickly. "Nothing."

The big man looked sharply at him. "Freddy got lucky this morning," he said. "Caught a big striper. We're going up to enter it now. Come on," he said, giving Freddy a push. "Let's go."

"Where's the fish?" I asked.

Freddy looked down. The big man said brusquely, "In the cooler."

"Can I see it?" I asked.

"It's not here," said the big man, walking faster.

"Where did you catch it?" I called after them.

Freddy looked back and answered, "Right here. Gonna beat your daddy's record, I think, Ben."

I watched them disappear around the curve of the cliffs, fear and anger and disbelief rising together inside me.

I ran back to Jeff, gasping. "You won't believe what I just heard. Freddy Cobb and some other guy are cheating! They're entering a fish they caught six days ago and they're doing something to make it weigh more. Something with mercury."

Jeff reeled in his line slowly, staring at me. "No way," he said.

"Really," I answered. "I was walking around the point and I heard them talking before they realized I was there. Freddy was acting real nervous."

"What should we do?"

"We've got to stop them," I said.

"How?" asked Jeff.

"I don't know. Tell somebody."

"But how can we prove it?" asked Jeff.

"I don't know. Freddy was worried somebody would find the mercury. What would they do with mercury?

And how do they get mercury inside a fish, anyway?"

"Beats me," Jeff said with a shrug. "But I remember learning that mercury's real heavy."

"If they think they're going to beat my father's record with a doctored-up fish, they've got another think coming." I felt a fresh burst of anger at the idea. "Come on, let's go."

"Where?" asked Jeff.

"Let's go see if your parents will take us down to Chick's for the weigh-in tonight. We can tell somebody there what I heard," I said.

We put our gear in the cave, got our bikes, and pedaled furiously until we reached Jeff's house. The lights were out, and the pickup wasn't in the driveway.

"They're fishing," said Jeff. "There's no telling when they'll come back. They might fish most of the night."

"I'll call my house," I said.

The phone rang and rang. Mom must have already left to go out to dinner with Barry the Bozo.

"Shoot," I said, shaking my head with frustration.

The contest was set up so that fish could be entered twice a day, from eight o'clock to nine o'clock in the morning or evening. But derby headquarters was down at the other end of the island, more than fifteen miles away. There was no way Jeff and I could bike there in time, and no one was around to drive us.

"We might as well go back and keep fishing," Jeff said with a shrug. "We're not going to get down there tonight. Why don't we just wait until tomorrow? In the morning we can ask my parents what to do. Besides, maybe the judges will pay more attention to us if there are grown-ups along."

"I guess," I said reluctantly. It bugged me to think of those two getting away with their plan for even one night, to think of people believing Freddy Cobb had beaten Pop's record with his phony fish.

As we pulled up our bikes once again at the beach, I had an idea. "Jeff," I said, "we could go back and call Chick. He'll believe us."

"Man, I don't want to go all the way back home again. You can go if you want, but I want to do some fishing."

I stood uncertainly on the path. Maybe Jeff was right; we should do some fishing and wait until the morning to report what I'd heard. I followed him down the beach trail, but the fun had gone out of the night.

CHAPTER 6

Jeff and I fished for a while without much luck. The wind was blowing straight in off the ocean, making it hard to cast. We had missed the hour around sunset, which was a good time to catch stripers, but in another hour the tide would be changing. Hoping that it would bring in some fish, we decided to take a break to rest and eat.

The sky was dark and starry, and an almost-full moon was rising at our backs. I gathered some driftwood and made a fire. We sat on either side of it, eating our sandwiches and looking out at the water.

"Right now those guys are probably weighing in that fish," I said with disgust. "I hope they get caught."

"Old man McDonough has been judging these contests for a long time," said Jeff. "It'd be tough to get something past him."

"Yeah," I said, but in my mind I saw the confident

sneer on the face of the big man. He hadn't seemed worried about getting caught.

We stared silently at the waves. The night wasn't turning out the way I had expected. For one thing, I kept worrying that my mother would find out I was fishing all night with Jeff. But worse was the thought of Freddy and his friend winning the derby with their bogus fish. I kept imagining the scene down at headquarters: Freddy smiling and shaking hands, people clapping as his name replaced my father's on the big board.

"How did they keep the fish alive?" I wondered out loud. "They said they'd had it for six days."

"There's lots of ways, I guess," said Jeff thoughtfully.

"Like what?" I asked. "It would die on a stringer."

"Well, they could have kept it alive in a bait tank. Or in one of the saltwater ponds. But they'd definitely have to keep it alive. Old man McDonough can tell if a fish has been dead for more than a day."

"Yeah."

"He'll catch those guys," Jeff said, "one way or another."

"I hope so," I said. We ate for a moment in silence.

"I told my dad about the cave," I confessed suddenly to Jeff. "And guess what? He knew about it. It was his secret place when he was a kid, too. Remind me, and I'll show you his initials carved on the back wall."

"Cool," said Jeff.

"You're not mad that I told?" I asked.

Jeff shook his head. A few minutes went by. I was thinking about Pop, and I guess Jeff was, too. He said, "Remember the time you and your dad came with us when we went out to Noman's in our boat, and the engine conked out and the radio didn't work, either? We thought we were going to spend the night in the boat without any food or anything, until your dad fixed the engine with some junk out of the tackle box. My dad still talks about that."

I nodded proudly, remembering. Then I said, "And now we have Barry the Bozo, who probably couldn't find his way out of his Cadillac if the doors were locked. He actually wanted to go out and dig worms for striper bait. I don't know how my mother can stand him."

Jeff seemed to hesitate and shifted on the sand. "My mom says Barry's nice, even if he's different from your dad."

I snorted.

"She says it's good your mom is seeing Barry. Mom said maybe it'll help her, you know, get over your dad."

"Get over him!" I said with disgust. Maybe Mom could "get over" Pop. She could spend all her time with stupid Barry Lester, acting as if she'd forgotten about Pop. But I couldn't.

All of a sudden I could hear Mr. Nixon, the school psychologist Mom had made me talk to. I could hear his voice, sounding real sorrowful, saying, "Life gives us some tough knocks sometimes, Ben, and we just have to move on." Sure, just move on—as if Pop had never existed. There were times when I half expected to see him at the breakfast table, finishing his coffee and pulling on his high black boots and yellow slicker pants. Then would come the slow, dark realization that nothing was the way it used to be, that I'd never see Pop again.

I started to tell Jeff about it, but I stopped, feeling embarrassed. We didn't usually talk about stuff like that. I was glad it was nighttime so Jeff couldn't see my face. Instead I said, "Now Mom acts like fishing is some kind of dirty word."

"Sometimes I think about what it would be like if my dad died, and I . . . I . . . " Jeff stopped, shaking his head.

I felt as if I had a number-three lead sinker stuck in my throat. I couldn't answer.

The wind had died down, and in the silence between waves I heard a soft *pop*.

"Did you hear that?" Jeff asked excitedly.

I was already on my feet. "That was a striper if I ever heard one," I said, running to get my rod. Jeff was right behind me. We stood together at the water's edge, barely breathing, listening. There it was again, the unmistakable sound of a fish feeding on the surface. I felt a shiver of anticipation, and my eyes scanned the water in the direction of the sound. The moon was just high enough for each wave to catch a little light and carry it in to shore.

"There," I whispered to Jeff, pointing with my rod.

We watched as, once again, the dark shape of a fish appeared above the surface. We didn't start casting right away, but stood watching and listening.

"I think there's more than one," Jeff whispered back. "They seem to keep feeding in the same place."

"A bunch of bait must have come in with the tide," I said. "Let's get 'em."

Jeff walked a few yards to the left, and I moved to the right. We began casting.

On my first cast, I saw a swirl near my lure as a fish followed it, then swam away. "I had a look," I called softly to Jeff. Reeling in slowly, I kept my eyes on the water and saw another fish. I cast again, in front of where I'd seen it. The lure plopped into the water, and I began working it in, giving it what I hoped was an irresistible wiggle. Boom! The fish took it and started swimming hard out to sea. It felt like a good one.

Out of the corner of my eye, I saw Jeff give me the thumbs-up sign before he cast again. I took my time, playing the fish, letting it take out line when it wanted to and pumping and reeling when it rested. Finally I brought it in to shore. It was a striper, all right. Jeff came over to have a look.

"Nice fish," he said.

"A beauty, but not big enough to enter. Do you

think your parents would want it to eat?" I didn't mention what Jeff already knew, that I didn't bother taking fish home anymore, since my mother hadn't cooked any in a year.

"They'll probably catch something themselves," Jeff said.

"I'll release it," I said. Pop's rule had always been: Take what you need for food, let the rest go free for another day. Carefully I removed the hook from the fish's mouth, held it in the water until I felt its strength return, and let it go, the way Pop had taught me. "Go get bigger and make lots of babies," I called to it. Then, feeling silly, I looked around to see if Jeff had heard me.

"You talk to fish, Daggett?" As he moved back up the beach, he added, "I thought I was the only one crazy enough to do that."

The fishing was great for the next few hours. It seemed that either Jeff or I had one on all the time.

At three o'clock in the morning, we decided to quit and go to Jeff's house so that we'd be sure to see his parents before they went back out in the boat. Between us we had caught and released five more fairly good-sized stripers, plus three or four bluefish. The fishing had been so much fun that I'd almost forgotten what I'd seen and heard earlier. But as Jeff and I biked down the darkened road, I could think of nothing except making sure that Freddy Cobb and his friend didn't get away with their plan to win the derby.

CHAPTER 7

When we got to Jeff's house, his parents were in bed, so Jeff went to his room to get a little sleep, and I curled up on the couch in the living room.

"Morning, Ben," Mrs. Manning said as she came out of the kitchen with a cup of coffee in one hand and a cup of cocoa in the other. "How did you two do?" she asked, handing me the cocoa.

"Thanks, Mrs. Manning," I said, sitting up sleepily. "We did okay. Five nice stripers and some blues. How about you?"

"We had about an hour of really good action out by Noman's," she replied. "I caught a big blue, big enough that I wanted to enter it. We went down to headquarters for the weigh-in, and you'll never guess—"

All at once I was wide awake. "Freddy Cobb!" I cried. "Did he show up?"

"Well, yes," said Mrs. Manning, looking surprised. "How did you know?"

I jumped up from the couch. "He's cheating! Freddy and another guy. I heard them! They caught a fish six days ago and did something with mercury to make it weigh more and they're going to try to win the prize money with it. They—"

"Hold on, Ben," said Mrs. Manning, gently touching my arm. "Are you still dreaming?"

"No! I heard them talking on the beach."

"But, Ben," said Mrs. Manning, "we were there at the weigh-in. We saw the fish. Mr. McDonough was there, and he didn't seem to find anything amiss. Are you sure about this?"

"Yes," I said. "We've got to go and tell them."

Mrs. Manning's face looked grave. "Joe," she called to her husband. "You'd better come hear this."

Mr. Manning came into the living room, followed by Jeff. I told the whole story of what I had seen and heard the day before.

Mr. Manning shook his head in disbelief. "I've heard of things like that happening in other fishing contests," he said, "but never here. I can't believe Freddy let himself be a part of something like this."

"He seemed pretty worried, but the other guy told him to just relax. He said no one would ever find the mercury, even if they gutted the fish," I said. "Did they gut it?"

"No," answered Jeff's mother. "Freddy took it home with him. There seemed no reason to suspect foul play.

Mr. McDonough handled the fish, weighed it, measured it and so forth, and—"

"How much did it weigh?" I asked loudly.

I saw Mr. and Mrs. Manning look at each other uneasily.

"How much?" I asked again, and my voice didn't sound like my own.

"Sixty-six pounds, eleven ounces," Mr. Manning answered in a low voice.

Sixty-six pounds, eleven ounces. Four ounces more than my father's record.

I couldn't speak.

Mr. Manning put his hand on my shoulder. "I'm sorry, Ben. But we'll go right down there. We'll talk to Mr. McDonough as soon as headquarters opens."

"Right now I think we should all have some pancakes," said Mrs. Manning, guiding me to the kitchen table.

All through breakfast I sat in a daze, not hearing much of what Jeff and his parents said about the previous night's fishing or about Freddy and his fish. No one spoke as we drove down-island to the Edgartown dock and waited for the doors to open at derby headquarters.

Walking in, I looked immediately toward the front of the room, at the chalkboard where the current derby winner was posted each day. Freddy Cobb's name was written in first place. Otis Pritchard, one of the derby officials, was standing on a stool in front of the official board, where island records were carved. He had placed a strip of masking tape over my father's name, and was about to start writing on it with a Magic Marker.

"Not so fast, Otis," said Mr. Manning. "We have a little problem we need to talk about."

"What's that, Joe? Don't tell me you caught something bigger this morning?" asked Otis, winking at me.

"No, it's not that," said Mr. Manning. "But I think you'd better come down off that stool and listen to Ben."

Otis came over to where we were standing. Mr. McDonough and Lucy Silva, the two other officials, joined us.

"What's this all about?" asked Lucy.

I told my story again.

"Mercury?" repeated Otis, bewildered.

"I've heard of keeping fish alive to enter in a contest later," said Lucy, "but I've never heard about this mercury business."

Mr. McDonough was looking very worried. "I've read about it. Apparently, it's not that difficult," he said, "but I don't know exactly how it works, either. Freddy's fish felt normal. Are you sure about what you heard, Ben?" he asked.

I nodded.

Mr. McDonough gazed into space. "It did occur to

me," he said slowly, "that the fish wasn't as long as the record fish, yet it weighed more. But I didn't think too much about it. It was a fine, healthy-looking fish. I had no reason to suspect Freddy Cobb. Why, he's lived on this island all his life. Why would he want to pull a damn fool stunt like this?"

"I can think of ten thousand reasons," said Lucy dryly.

"Freddy entered the fish," said Otis, turning to me, "but you said there were two men. Who was the other one?"

"I don't know," I answered. "I've never seen him before. But it seemed like—" I hesitated, not sure what to say.

"What, Ben?" asked Mrs. Manning. "It might be important."

"Well, Freddy was nervous and scared. And it seemed like the other guy was sort of—in charge. Like he was telling Freddy what to do. At least, that's the way it seemed."

"Interesting," said Otis. "We'll have to see if we can find out who that fellow was."

"This is terrible," said Lucy. "Cheating when there's ten thousand dollars at stake is a real crime. What are we going to do?"

"The only thing we can do is contact Freddy and ask him to bring the fish back and let us examine it," said Mr. McDonough.

"The big guy told him to get rid of it," I said.

"That's what I was afraid of," said Mr. McDonough. "If there really is foul play going on here, Freddy won't give us another look at that fish. And if that's the case, well, our hands may be tied."

I couldn't believe it. "You mean you might let him get away with it?" I asked.

"I'm not sure what else we can do, Ben," said Mr. McDonough. "If you had gotten this information to us last night, we'd have been able to follow up on it. But without the fish, it's your word against his. I believe you, son, don't get me wrong. But without any proof, I may be hard put to take that first place away from Freddy Cobb."

"Unless somebody else catches a bigger fish," Lucy added, looking at me.

"Well, of course," said Mr. McDonough. The tone of his voice made it clear what he thought were the chances of *that* happening.

CHAPTER 8

On the way home, Mr. Manning looked at me in the rearview mirror and said, "If this thing doesn't get straightened out, Ben, it'll be a real sad thing to see your father's record beaten by those two lowlifes. But this is a small island. Word will get around real quick about Freddy's tricks, and everyone will know who *really* holds the record. It won't matter what the big board says."

"I guess so," I said dully. Mr. Manning was right. All the fishermen would know the truth before long. But Pop's name had been on that board since before I was born. People had pointed it out to me before I could even read.

"You know something, Ben?" asked Jeff's mother. "I've been thinking. That record never seemed to matter much to your father. Other people talked about Jack Daggett's big fish, but not Jack."

I didn't say anything. I knew she was trying to make me feel better, but she didn't understand. Pop's record *did* matter. It mattered to me.

As we neared home, Mrs. Manning turned around and said, "Boys, why don't the two of you come out with us in the boat? We'll pack a lot of food and make a day of it. We can stay out just as long as we please. How does that sound?"

Jeff looked at me, his eyebrows raised. I felt real weird. Sort of jumpy and mad and full of a jittery kind of energy. The back of my neck was prickly, my eyes were hot, and something in my chest was fluttering around like crazy. I knew I had to *do* something. I didn't know what, but I couldn't sit in the boat all day with Jeff and his kind, sympathetic parents.

"Thanks," I said. "But I just feel like going home, I guess. You guys go out."

"Are you sure?" asked Jeff.

I nodded.

"We could fish off the beach instead," he offered.

I shook my head.

Mr. Manning turned down the sandy driveway to my house. Barry's Cadillac was parked by the door. Terrific.

"I'll call you later," said Jeff as I got out of the car.

"Okay. Get the big one," I said feebly.

When I walked into the house, Mom and Barry Lester were sitting at the kitchen table, talking.

"Why, hello, Ben," Mom said. "I thought you were out fishing."

"No," I answered.

"Well?" she asked, smiling at me. "How did you do?"

"Okay," I said.

"You caught some fish?"

"Yeah," I said.

"Any big ones?" she asked.

"Not really," I said.

Mom stopped asking questions and gave me a puzzled look, half worried and half irritated.

Barry's voice filled the silence. "Well, Ben, it's too bad you weren't with us last night. We had a delicious meal at the Rosehip Inn, didn't we, Kate?"

Ignoring Barry, I turned to Mom. "Maybe if you'd been home last night instead of out having your 'delicious meal,' Pop's name would still be up on the board. If you'd been here to drive me to Edgartown, I'd have been able to stop Freddy!"

All the prickly, jumpy feelings were rushing to my head, and I could feel my face growing red and my voice growing louder and louder. "But you don't care! Nobody cares except me! You just want to move on and forget all about Pop. Well, I won't forget him. Ever!"

Whatever had been fluttering around in my chest was in my throat, threatening to choke me, and I struggled to catch my breath. Damn it! I was crying in front of Barry Lester. Turning, I ran up the stairs to my room, slammed the door, and fell face down on the bed.

There were anxious murmurings from downstairs. The back door opened and closed. I heard the crunch of Barry's tires backing down the driveway. After a long silence, there was a knock at my bedroom door. "Ben, I need to talk to you." It was Mom's no-nonsense voice, but it sounded different, kind of shaky.

"Door's open," I mumbled into my pillow.

"I can't hear you."

I turned over and sat up on the bed. "The door's open," I said in a hard voice.

Mom walked in and stood by the bed. "I'd like to know what that was all about, Ben," she said.

I couldn't think of how to begin explaining.

"What is all this about your father?"

I couldn't answer.

"Ben, help me here. What's going on? Who's Freddy?"

That question I could answer. "Freddy Cobb. He fishes with Captain Norton on the *Aquinnah.*"

"Well? What about him?" Mom reached over to my dresser, got a tissue, and handed it to me. "What about Freddy Cobb?" she asked again while I blew my nose and took a deep breath.

"He cheated," I said. "He entered a fish he caught

before the derby opened, and he added mercury to it so it weighed four ounces more than Pop's record fish. And it looks like he's going to get away with it."

Mom asked more questions and I answered briefly, not looking at her.

"And this is my fault because I went out to dinner and couldn't give you a ride to Edgartown?" she asked.

I shrugged. I knew that was unfair, but I didn't care. Part of me wanted to hurt her.

She sat down on the edge of the bed and touched my arm. I pulled it away.

"Ben, why are you so angry with me?" she asked. "Do you really think I've forgotten your father?"

I didn't answer. Wasn't Barry Lester proof of that?

"Maybe this is hard for you to understand," she said, "but I loved your father very much. I still do. As much as you do. Of course it's a different kind of love between a husband and wife than between a father and son. But I miss him every single day, Ben, just as you do. For a while I couldn't bear living on this island. I couldn't bear having to look at the sea. I know you think I'm silly about it, but I'm terrified that something will happen to you, too, and I know I couldn't stand that. I'm trying hard not to hold you too close, and I'm not doing a very good job. I'm also trying to make some kind of a normal life for us, whatever that means, and I don't seem to be doing very well at that, either."

She stopped. I could tell she was crying. I wanted to put my arms around her and cry, too, but the part of me that wanted to do that felt far away and frozen.

Mom got up, got herself a tissue, and kept talking. "I think you owe Barry an apology. He doesn't deserve the way you've treated him. He's not trying to take your father's place, Ben. No one can do that. He just wants to be our friend. And I, for one, can use a friend. He's a good man, Ben. I wish you could see that."

There was another long silence. My mind was filled with a hundred things, but how can you say a hundred things at once? There's no place to start.

Mom left quietly, closing the door behind her. After a while I heard noises in the kitchen. Mom knocked and asked if I wanted lunch. I said no. Later, I made myself a sandwich for dinner and went back to my room. I lay on my back as the sky outside grew dark. I heard the lights click off, Mom's footsteps come up the stairs, her door close. Then everything grew quiet, except for the voice in my head that kept repeating, It's not fair, it's not fair, it's not fair.

Nothing was fair: not having to apologize to Barry Lester, not Freddy Cobb getting away with cheating, not Pop dying in a hurricane called Lois. Without Pop, Mom and I weren't the same. We walked around the house treating each other almost like strangers, as if we didn't know how to act without him there.

Mom didn't care how I felt about Barry the Bozo.

And nothing I did would ever bring Pop back. But, I thought, I didn't have to lie there and let Freddy and his friend steal Pop's place on the big board.

I got out of bed, crept down the stairs, and stepped out the kitchen door into the night.

CHAPTER 9

The night was clear and the moon was just one day from being full, so I could see pretty well as I pedaled hard down the Lobsterville Beach road. Cars and jeeps belonging to fishermen were parked all along the beach, and over the low dunes I could see the lights from their lanterns. The road ended at West Basin, where twice a day the tide flowed from the sea through a narrow channel into a huge saltwater pond and back again.

On the other side of the channel was Menemsha Harbor. That was where the big fishing boats, including the *Aquinnah*, docked. I didn't have a plan. But Freddy Cobb worked on the *Aquinnah*, and sometimes the crews from the commercial boats would hang around at the docks, playing cards and telling stories. If Freddy was there, I'd find him.

I stashed my bike in the tangle of beach plums and

searched the row of overturned dinghies on the shore, looking for the one that belonged to Jeff's father. Quickly I turned it right side up, dragged it down to the water, stepped in, and began to row. Hard. The tide was still coming in, through the narrow channel and up into the pond. I had crossed the channel many times and knew that I had to row not only across, but against the tide. The channel was always treacherous, but especially on the outgoing tide, when a mistake meant you would be swept out into the open waters of Vineyard Sound.

There were still some fishermen casting from the stone jetties on either side of the channel, and I was careful to stay away from their lures. Sweating from exertion, I pulled the boat up onto the Menemsha shore, above the high-tide mark. I didn't think I'd be very long, but I knew better than to leave a boat where the tide could reach it. It was something Pop had taught me when I was just a little kid.

I walked along the dock, past the big luxury boats belonging to the tourists, and into the lighted area of Squid Row. The bait shop was closed, but Pete Vanderhoop, the harbormaster, was sitting on the bench outside.

"Ben Daggett, is that you?" he called.

"Hi, Pete. It's me, all right," I answered.

"Where were you today?" he asked. "The albacore were in the channel thick as mullet. Bonito, too."

Usually the news would have made me perk right up. Albies and bonito were really fun to catch. But I had other things on my mind.

"Is the *Aquinnah* around?" I asked.

"Right in her usual berth," answered Pete. He looked at me curiously. "Why?"

"I'm looking for Freddy Cobb," I said, trying to sound casual.

"Freddy's a mighty popular fellow tonight," Pete observed, holding a match to his pipe.

I stopped walking. "What do you mean?"

"You're the third person who's come looking for Freddy," said Pete.

"Who else?" I asked.

Pete shrugged. "Didn't know either of 'em," he said. "Guess Freddy's a real celebrity now that he caught himself a big fish."

I scowled. "Right."

"Too bad, Ben," said Pete. "About your father's record, I mean. I heard Freddy's fish was bigger."

"Don't be too sure about that, Pete," I said. I walked away before I could say anything else.

I headed down the dock to where the commercial boats rocked in their berths like huge, resting whales. These weren't pleasure boats, but hardworking iron giants, smelling pungently of fish and tar and diesel fuel. There were no lights here, and the moon had passed behind a cloud.

In the dark shadows I saw strange shapes that made my heart start to flutter. That's just an oil drum, I told myself. And that's a pile of lobster traps. Come on, you've been here a hundred times before.

Ahead I could see the outline of the *Aquinnah*, looking dark and deserted in its place at the end of the pier. You dope, I told myself. Freddy's not here. No one's here. What did you think you were going to do, anyway, catch him red-handed with the fish and make him confess? Make him *apologize*? I almost laughed out loud at my foolishness.

Approaching the *Aquinnah*, I looked for a light below decks, or for any sign of life. Nothing. I was about to turn and leave when I saw the red glow of a cigarette near the stern. I stared while the cigarette moved and burned brighter as someone took a long, slow drag. For a moment I could see the features of the smoker's face, but not well enough to recognize them. Sitting in the dark, whoever it was must have seen me and heard me coming, but he didn't speak. There was something creepy about the way he sat there, watching me, not saying a word.

I decided to take a chance. "Freddy?" I called.

There was a long pause. Then a low voice growled, "Who wants to know?"

The voice was familiar, but I couldn't place it. Some instinct warned me not to say my name. "Just a friend," I said quickly, and turned to go.

I saw the cigarette fly overboard and heard it hit the water with a hiss. Then a dark shadow emerged from the other shadows on deck and began moving toward me. Fast.

I began to run. A hand grabbed the hood of my windbreaker and the nylon pulled against my throat, choking me. I stopped running and turned to see the big man who'd been at the beach with Freddy, still holding onto my hood. I didn't speak as he looked me over carefully.

"You," he said in that same low growl. " 'Just a friend,' eh? From what I hear, you've been trying to cause a little trouble for Freddy. Now, that's not what I'd call friendly, would you?" He pulled my face closer to his. "Well, would you?"

"You cheater!" I shouted. "Let go of me!"

"You're not stupid, are you? You're not going to mess things up for our friend Freddy, now are you?" he asked in a quiet voice that was worse than any shout. "Because if you are—"

"Let *go,*" I said again, and at the same time I brought the heel of my sneaker down hard on the arch of his foot. Taking advantage of his surprise and pain, I wriggled free of his grasp and began to run down the dock toward the lights at Squid Row.

"You little—"

Heavy footsteps followed me down the dock, but I didn't look back. "Pete!" I called, straining to see if the harbormaster was still sitting on the bench. He was gone. There's always somebody hanging around the docks, I thought wildly, especially during the derby. Where is everybody?

"Hey, kid," I heard the big man call, not far behind me, as I raced past the bait shop and out the long pier toward the channel. Running along the jetty made of huge, irregularly shaped rocks, my feet didn't falter. I'd run along that jetty a thousand times. I heard the big man stumble and curse loudly. I jumped off the jetty onto the sandy beach and headed for the dinghy.

With part of my mind I noticed that the tide had changed and was now on its way out. Grunting with effort, I dragged the little boat toward the water, which was pouring rapidly through the channel on its way to the open ocean.

I could hear the *plop* as the big man jumped from the jetty onto the sand and the crunch of his footsteps growing nearer. Without waiting to seat the oars, I hopped into the dinghy and pushed off. But the boat didn't float: Because of the falling tide, the water was shallower than I had thought. I grabbed an oar, dug it into the sand, and pushed with all my might. As the big man drew close, I could hear his harsh breathing in the still night. "Come *on*," I whispered, nearly sobbing now with fear and frustration. Finally I felt the boat lift free of the beach, and immediately the rapidly rushing water pulled me away from shore and into the channel. I had a brief glimpse of the big man's arm reaching for the gunwale as I made my escape.

But I didn't have time for relief. Grabbing for the oars, I fumbled in the darkness, trying to fit them into the oarlocks. The left one fell in with a solid clunk, but I couldn't make the right one fit. When it finally went in, I looked up to get my bearings.

I was more than halfway down the channel, being carried by the fast, dark water out into the open sea.

CHAPTER 10

Okay, I told myself. Don't panic. I knew it was impossible to row against the tide all the way back up the channel. The best thing was to go with it, out through the mouth, into the ocean. Once I was out of the rip created by the huge rush of water through the narrow neck of the channel, I could row along the shore and then head straight in to Lobsterville Beach.

For a minute I thought I heard Pop's voice. That's right, Ben. Don't try to fight the tide. Just use the oars to keep the boat straight. Keep your head and you'll be fine.

The clouds had cleared away, and in the moonlight I could see the big green bell buoy that marked the entrance to the harbor, and I could hear its mournful clang. When I was clear of the two huge stone jetties on either side of the channel, I began to row as hard as I could. The wind was from the west, which wasn't really helping me, but at least it wasn't a south wind, which would have blown me straight out from the shore. I angled the boat toward the beach and concentrated on pulling, pulling, pulling on the oars.

Looking over my shoulder, I saw the outline of the dunes getting closer, and at last I heard the scrape of the hull on the sand. I dragged the dinghy way up onto the dunes, turned it over, and hid the oars underneath it. Later I'd explain to the Mannings how it got there.

For a while, I'd been afraid the big man might steal a dinghy from the harbor and follow me, but he hadn't. If he was really after me, it would take him at least twenty minutes to drive from the harbor, around the big pond, and down the Lobsterville Beach road. How long had it taken me to get to shore? It had seemed like hours, but was probably more like . . . twenty minutes, I thought sickly.

There were a few jeeps and pickups parked at the West Basin lot. Could he be in one of them, waiting?

I crept along the dunes, looking for any sign of movement. I came to the thicket of beach-plum bushes where I'd left my bike. I began riding up the road. If I see headlights coming, I thought, I'll jump off and hide in the bushes.

As I rode, I tried to make sense of what had happened. If I'd had any doubt that Freddy and the big man were up to something, it was gone now. Why else would he have chased me, if not to stop me from telling what I knew? But why had he been lurking, hidden, aboard the *Aquinnah*? Where was Freddy?

Pete had said there were two other people looking for Freddy besides me. The big man must have been one of them. Who was the other? And why, if they were in on this together, didn't the big man know where Freddy was?

My brain felt tired from all the questions, but the rest of me was wide awake, alert. I didn't have a watch on, but looking at the moon, I judged it to be about two o'clock in the morning. I thought about going home. If Mom had discovered I was missing, she'd be worried sick. But once she realized I was all right, she'd be furious with me for sneaking out.

I decided not to go home. If I was already in trouble, I could wait to hear about it. I'll bike to Edgartown, I thought, to derby headquarters. That way I'll be there when they open in the morning, and I'll tell them what happened.

Then Freddy and his friend would have some explaining to do.

CHAPTER 11

The problem with a small island is that there aren't many roads. If the big man was driving around looking for me, he wouldn't have many places to look. There isn't much traffic, either, at two o'clock in the morning. But each set of headlights set my heart pounding and sent me leaping into the bushes on the side of the road, dragging my bike in after me. I'd be lucky if I didn't have poison ivy from head to toe before the night was over.

After about forty minutes, I began to relax and enjoy the ride. There was something exciting about riding silently down the narrow winding road alone in the darkness, and even with thoughts of the big man in my mind, it was kind of peaceful. The scrubby oak trees grew together over the road, so it seemed as if I were zooming through a tunnel. At times the view opened up, and I could see the moonlight sparkling on the water. I heard the scratchy chirp of the crickets and the occasional flat *kr-a-a-k* of a night heron. Once an owl floated silently along beside me. A while later, a family of skunks paraded across the road. To my relief, they ignored me completely.

The sky was turning bright in the east as I rolled into Edgartown and pedaled slowly to the docks. The coming of daylight made me feel safer, but it did nothing to stop the fierce noises coming from my stomach. I was starving. A fisherman passed me, heading for his boat, and I looked longingly at the big blueberry muffin and steaming cup in his hands. I dug through all my pockets, but didn't find any loose change. Chick would be opening the shop soon, and I contented myself with imagining the box of doughnuts that sat on the counter every morning.

Then I saw him.

The big man was leaning against the weathered shingles of Chick's Tackle Shop, his head back, smoking. At first glance, he looked relaxed and casual, an early riser watching the streets and docks coming to life. But I could see his hooded eyes looking sharply left and right. Was he looking for me?

If so, he hadn't seen me yet. I ducked into the doorway of a gift shop and tried to think what to do next. I wasn't sure what time it was, or when Chick opened in the mornings. But fishermen keep early hours, and I figured he'd open before the derby officials arrived at eight o'clock.

I decided to stay put and keep an eye out for Chick.

Chick was huge, bigger than the big man, and strong from many years spent at sea pulling commercial fishing nets. He'd been one of my father's best friends. His large face was scarred and rough, and people who didn't know him found him frightening, but I knew better. He always had time for a joke or a kind word to me. When Pop was missing, Chick had spent days out in his boat, searching. And when they found Pop, people said Chick had broken down and cried like a baby.

I hid in the doorway, shivering as the sweat from biking dried on me in the damp, chilly morning air. I couldn't help watching the big man as he smoked, lighting each cigarette from the butt of the one before.

Finally I saw Chick's familiar blue truck pull into the lot across from the shop. Chick got out, a box of doughnuts in his hand. I ran from my hiding place, calling, "Chick!"

Chick turned. When he saw me, his face broke into a crooked grin.

"Ben! What brings you here so early? You need more of those blue poppers?"

"Chick! That guy over there—" I pointed to where the big man had been standing.

He was gone.

I ran to the shop and looked around the corner and up and down the docks, but there was no sign of him.

Chick was behind me. "Ben? What's going on?"

"There was a man there, just a minute ago. Last

night he chased me and I got away, but he was here waiting for me. At least I think that's what he was doing. He's the guy who's cheating with Freddy and—"

"Everyone's talking about that," said Chick. "So it's true?"

"I overheard them say it," I told him. "And he—the big guy—knows that I know, and must have found out that I told, and that's why he was looking for me."

"You say he chased you?" Chick asked, his face growing dark and angry looking.

I nodded.

"What does he want with you?"

I shrugged. "I guess he wants to stop me from saying anything more. I think he's afraid of something going wrong before they get the prize money. I think he was looking for Freddy last night, too."

"Looking for Freddy, *too*? Who else was looking for Freddy?" asked Chick.

"Well, I was," I answered. "And maybe somebody else."

"Ben, does your mother know where you've been?"

I looked away. "No."

"All right. First things first."

I looked hopefully at the doughnuts. Chick laughed. "Here," he said, handing me the box. "Eat 'em all. You look like you need 'em. What I meant was, the first thing I want you to do is call your mother. Then we'll decide what to do about the rest of this."

Chick opened the shop, turned on the lights, and

pointed to the phone. "I'll heat up some water for hot chocolate," he said.

I hadn't really thought about what I was going to say, and for a moment, when my mother answered, sounding worried and scared, I couldn't speak.

"Hi, Mom. It's me."

"Ben," I heard her say. Then there was silence except for the sound of her crying.

"I'm at Chick's, Mom," I said. "I'm okay, honest."

I heard her swallow and sniffle. Then she asked, "Where have you been?" Her voice went way up on the *been*. "I've been so worried. I tried to reach Barry—I thought he could help me find you—but he wasn't home."

Barry. I didn't feel like talking about Barry.

"Where were you?" she asked again. "Were you out all night?"

"Most of it, I guess," I said. "I was looking for Freddy."

I tried to explain, but it wasn't easy. Mom was upset, and I could tell she didn't know whether to be mad at me or glad that I was safe. She said she was coming to Chick's to get me, and I hung up.

While I'd been on the phone, the derby officials had begun to arrive, and a hushed discussion was going on in the room adjoining the tackle shop.

I walked over in time to hear Mr. McDonough explain, "The judge said we could get a search warrant based on the fact that the story Ben is telling sounds credible. The problem is, the search warrant has to be for a specific place: Freddy's truck, for instance, or his house. But we don't really know where to look for the fish. Do you have any idea, Ben?" he asked, turning to me.

I shook my head. "I couldn't even find Freddy," I said. "I have no idea what he did with the fish."

"Apparently no one can find Freddy," said Chick.

"We're hoping he'll turn up at the awards ceremony tonight," said Lucy Silva. "After he's gone to so much trouble to win, I can't imagine he won't show up to claim the money."

"And then you'll arrest him?" I asked.

Everyone looked uncomfortable. "Well, Ben," said Mr. McDonough, "without evidence to prove that Freddy cheated, we can't withhold the prize. Of course, if evidence turns up later, we'll be able to prosecute and so on. But for right now, it looks as if Freddy's going to get away with it."

"What about this other guy?" asked Chick, his deep voice angry. "The one who chased Ben? He's in on it, too."

"I suppose you and your mother should stop at the police station and file a complaint," said Mr. McDonough. "Tell them the whole story. Get it on the record. Maybe they can do something about it. Did he actually hurt you, Ben?"

"No," I said. "He just grabbed my hood. I got away and then he chased me." Now, in the light of day, it was hard to tell if the threat of violence I'd felt from the big man was as real as it had seemed. "But he was here this morning. And he disappeared when Chick came."

Mr. McDonough looked around uneasily, as if he expected to see the big man lurking in a corner.

Through the window I saw my mother's car pull up. "Well, my mom's here," I said. "I've got to go. Thanks, Chick . . ."

Chick reached over and held my shoulder tight. "On the board at Chick's," he said, "Jack Daggett's name is staying on top. No matter what happens."

He was looking right into my eyes, and I had the feeling that he understood how I felt, even if nobody else did.

As I turned to go, Mr. McDonough called, "You be sure to tell your mother about stopping by the police station, son."

"Okay," I said, but I'd already decided not to do that. Why get Mom more upset than she already was? And it sounded as if nobody could do anything about Freddy and his friend, anyway. Not the judge, not the police, not the derby officials, not even Chick. All I'd done was get Mom worried, and I'd accomplished nothing. If Pop were alive, he'd know what to do, I was sure of it. But Pop was dead—and so was his record.

I got into the car.

CHAPTER 12

Mom looked horrible. Her eyes were red with big black circles under them, and her skin looked all blotchy. Her mouth shook as she said, "I don't know what to do with you anymore, Ben. I don't know what to say. I—" She stopped talking and looked away from me, out the window.

I felt awful.

"I think you need your father now, Ben, and I don't know what to do about that. I can't be both mother and father to you. People talk about that, but I don't know what it means. I can't do it." She turned to me. "I'm trying, Ben, but I don't know what you want from me."

"I'm sorry," I said.

Mom waited, her eyes searching my face.

"About last night . . . I thought I could find Freddy and maybe fix everything. I . . . " My voice trailed off, and I felt foolish. "It was a dumb idea. I didn't mean to get you worried. It just seemed like something I had to do."

Mom put the car in gear and began to drive slowly out of town. After a moment she said, "Well, *I'm* sorry about your dad's record, since it seems to mean so much to you. I didn't really understand that. I guess when I think of him, I think about other things. Like the way he looked when he was out fishing, his hair plastered with salt spray, and his teeth so white against his skin. And the way he made me feel . . . so good. . . . Nobody could make me laugh like your father." She laughed, but it wasn't the loud, reckless whoop I used to hear from the kitchen when Pop was there. It made me feel worse, hearing that sad, soft sound. Pop used to make her laugh, and all I did was make everything harder for her.

"Yeah," I said. "I know."

We rode along in silence for a while. Then Mom said, "Don't ever do that again, Ben. Don't ever go out at night like that without telling me. Promise me."

"I promise," I said.

"And I promise to stop . . . clinging so tight. I couldn't bear to lose you, too, Ben. Do you understand?"

"Yes," I said, and I did.

"Well, then," she went on, "what do you want to do today? It's still early."

"Eat," I said promptly.

Mom smiled. "All day?" she asked.

"Maybe." I smiled, too. "And then, if it's okay, I want to go back out fishing. It's the last day and maybe—well, Lucy Silva said one way to fix Freddy would be to catch a bigger fish. I know it's stupid, but I feel like trying, anyway."

I stopped. Would she understand, or was I just giving her something else to worry about?

"Okay," she said. "I can see wanting to finish whatever it is you've started."

I didn't even know I was going to say it, but suddenly I heard myself ask, "Do you want to come with me?"

She looked at me, surprised. Then she shook her head. "No. Not today, Ben. Not yet." She paused. "But ask me again someday, will you?"

"Sure."

"Someday I'll be ready."

"Okay," I said.

"The derby's over tonight at six o'clock, right?" she asked.

"Right," I answered. It would be starting to get dark by then, so I added, "I'll come home right after."

"I'll take you down to Chick's for the final weigh-in and awards, if you like," Mom offered. "Or maybe you'd rather not."

I thought about it. I didn't really know why, but I wanted to see the whole thing through, even if it meant watching Freddy and his friend walk off with the prize.

"No, let's go," I said.

After a huge breakfast of fried eggs and ham, home fries and Mom's muffins, I got out the sliced turkey and bread and started making myself a sandwich for lunch.

"Better make two," said Mom, smiling. "We wouldn't want you to go hungry."

"Good idea." I put the sandwiches in my pack, along with a couple boxes of juice, and then I kissed Mom good-bye, something I hadn't done in a long time.

"See you a little after six," I promised.

"Good luck," she said. "And be ca—" She stopped herself. "Good luck," she repeated. "Have fun."

CHAPTER 13

Climbing the cliffs to the cave, I thought briefly of the big man. He could be around, I supposed, but I wasn't worried. He must have figured out by now that I was no threat to him anymore. He and Freddy had won.

I checked the conditions. Southwest wind. Good. I wouldn't have to cast against it, but there was enough chop on the water to keep the fish from being nervous. Tide was on the way out. That was good, too. It would be changing, coming in, just about twilight.

In the cave, I ran my fingers over Pop's initials, carved in the grayish clay. JUD. Jackson Ulysses Daggett. He'd never liked the Ulysses part, saying it sounded too fancy for a fisherman. A man only needed two names, he said, a last name and a first name. He'd persuaded Mom to name me just Benjamin Daggett, nothing in the middle, which was fine with me.

I didn't pick up my fishing things right away, but sat on the floor of the cave on my sleeping bag, looking at Pop's initials. I took out my pocketknife and carved my initials, BD, next to Pop's. Benjamin Daggett. That's who I was, Jack Daggett's son. Then I picked up my rod and the red bucket and headed for the beach.

The fishing was slow. There were no birds working along the beach, but I kept casting mechanically, the repetitive motion and the continuous rhythm of the waves lulling me into a peaceful kind of trance. I took time out to eat my sandwiches, then began casting again.

Hours must have passed, because all at once I realized with a start that it was growing dark. In front of me the huge red sun was sinking into the sea, and behind me the full moon was rising against a blue-black, star-filled sky. The tide was rushing in. Tiny fingers of foam reached past my feet and receded, passing over hundreds of small rocks with a gentle rumble.

Casting, I had the oddest feeling of being somewhere I'd never been before. It was a place that was on the edge of everywhere, between day and night, and between land and sea.

I knew that it had to be getting close to six o'clock, but still I kept casting, caught by the glow of the sky and the strange feeling I had inside.

Suddenly there was a tug at the end of my line. It felt big and heavy and dead, like a log or an old tire.

I pulled back, trying to free my lure, but it was hard into something solid. Something big.

Great way to end the night, I thought, getting stuck on the bottom.

And then the bottom started to move.

Whatever was on the end of my line was heading steadily out to sea. It had to be a fish! A big, strong fish, from the feel of it. I hadn't seen anything. I hadn't heard anything. There had been no jumps, no wasted energy. Just the tug, and now my line spinning rapidly off the reel. If this kept up, I'd soon be out of line.

I tried to remember what to do in a situation like this. I listened for Pop's voice, and soon I heard it. Don't try to fight him now, he's too strong. Let him run. Let him get tired. Check your drag. You want just enough pressure to slow him down, make him work, but not so much that he breaks off.

There was nothing to do but hang on, so I did. My heart was beating so wildly that I felt as if my blood were rushing through me like the tide. I held on, watching the line spin out. There wasn't much left. I had to take a chance. I tightened the drag, hoping I could tire the fish out before it broke off or I ran out of line.

There were just a few more curls of line on the reel, and the fish was still swimming. I was preparing to feel its full strength, preparing for the disappointment when it came to the end of my line and broke free. But then it stopped. There was no pull on the end of the line. At first I thought the line *had* broken. Carefully I pulled back. It was still there! Resting.

I lifted the rod tip and lowered it, reeling as the tip came down. I lifted again and reeled. Again. I was gaining on the fish, but already my arms were tiring from the great weight of it. Lift. Reel. Lift. Reel.

Then the drag squealed loudly as the fish made another run, taking out almost all the line I had just gained. Again it stopped to rest. Again I worked it in, reeling and lifting for what seemed like hours.

Suddenly, out beyond the waves, I saw it for the first time. A huge shape broke the surface and struggled briefly, then disappeared. It was gigantic. It was the biggest fish I'd ever seen. In a sudden panic I was sure I'd never get this fish in. I began thinking of all the things that could go wrong: A careless knot could come undone, a weak spot in the line could snap, the hook could straighten out or break, the fish could make a quick run, the line could get wrapped around a clump of seaweed or a submerged piece of wood. . . .

Several more times we repeated our struggle, me lifting and reeling until my arms felt like lead, the fish somehow turning its head and heading out to sea once more. And then I could almost feel the fight go out of it. It was still heavy, hard to reel in, but I could tell that, for the moment, it was exhausted. Soon I could see it clearly in the shallow water, and I gasped.

This was the time when a fisherman had to be extra careful, the time when one false move could mean losing the fish. But I wasn't thinking about that.

I was looking at the biggest, strongest, most beautiful striped bass I had ever seen. It was almost as big as I was. My hands were shaking with fatigue and excitement as I watched it shining and flashing in the moonlit water, the black stripes standing out boldly against the silver-green sides, its eye, enormous, looking into mine and taking my measure.

I knew what I was supposed to do. I knew I should drag the fish high up onto the beach so it couldn't get away. But I just stood there, looking with wonder at this miracle that had appeared at my feet, this mysterious creature that had come to me from the sea. A distant part of my mind registered its length and girth, and knew it to be the biggest fish ever, bigger than Pop's. This was the fish that would beat Freddy's, that would win the derby and ten thousand dollars, the fish that could buy me a boat, the fish that would keep the Daggett name at the top of the record board.

But none of that seemed real. What was real was the power and beauty of this fish, and the amazing fact of its existence. This fish had come to me, Ben Daggett, from out of the vastness of the ocean, and I knew I wouldn't kill it. I didn't want to see this fish thrashing in the sand, gasping for breath, its brilliant colors fading as its life drained away.

Fish don't care about the record books. And at that moment, neither did I.

I reached down and lifted the hook from its mouth. I turned it until it was pointing out to sea, my hands touching its slippery smoothness. I pushed and pulled its great body into deeper water and gently moved it forward and back until its strength began to return. With a quick, shivering motion it suddenly broke from my grasp, flailed briefly in the shallows, then disappeared in the dark, swirling water.

I think I knelt there for a long time, the waves washing softly around my waders, my hands outstretched in a gesture of release. And I don't know how to explain it, but during those moments, or those seconds, or those hours, something happened. When I let the fish go, I felt a lot go along with it. The anger and pain I'd been living with since Pop died, the fear of living without him, even the rage about Freddy and the big man and their cheating seemed to disappear into the sea behind my fish.

I understood now why Pop's record hadn't mattered much to him. And I understood that Pop was a whole lot more to me than his name carved at the top of that board. For the first time, I knew that I still had the best parts of Pop. They were inside me, part of me, Ben Daggett.

I had the feeling that Pop was watching and that he was proud.

CHAPTER 14

As I walked down the beach, I looked out at the waves crashing over the rocks of Devil's Bridge and imagined my bass out there somewhere, swimming free. I felt strangely light, as if I could swim as easily as a fish, or fly if I wanted to. Approaching the dunes, I saw a figure moving toward me along the path. I wondered vaguely if it might be the big man, but I didn't feel afraid.

"Ben?"

"Mom? It's me."

We met on the path and began walking together.

"Sorry if I'm late," I said.

"I just thought I'd come down and see how you were doing."

"That's good, Mom."

"It's been a long time since I've been here," she said.

"I know."

"Do you still want to go to the award ceremony?" she asked.

"Sure," I said. I felt as if I had just awakened from a dream, and the dream still felt more real than the real world.

We got into the car, and as we drove to Edgartown I told Mom about the fish. At least I tried. It was hard to explain, but I think she knew what I was trying to say. When I finished she said quietly, "I guess you *are* a fisherman, after all."

I'd tell Jeff, too, of course, and Chick. They'd understand. But to most people it would probably sound like just another fish story about the big one that got away.

In town, we had to park about a mile away from Chick's and walk; nearly every parking space was filled. We walked past cars and jeeps and trucks with fishing rods on the roofs, rods sticking out the windows and bristling out of rod holders like porcupine quills.

Derby headquarters was jammed with fishermen, their families, and people who simply came to enjoy the show. It seemed as if everybody we knew was there. Children were running around, babies were crying, and everyone was talking fish, telling tales of the past three days' adventures and, of course, the good old days.

Mom and I inched through the crowd, saying hello to folks. I kept an eye out for Freddy and the big man, but didn't see them anywhere. Up near the makeshift stage I caught sight of Jeff and whistled to get his attention. He waved and motioned us forward. Then I saw a huddle of people standing near the judges' table. I recognized Mr. McDonough, Otis Pritchard, Lucy Silva, Chick, the Edgartown police chief, and—I couldn't believe my eyes—Barry Lester.

I elbowed Mom and pointed to the group. "What's he doing here?" I asked.

"I don't know," she said, looking surprised. "I haven't seen him since yesterday morning."

"Come on," I said, pulling her through the crowd.

"Hello, Kate. Hello, Ben," said a chorus of voices as we approached.

"What's going on?" I asked.

Everyone began to talk at once. Finally Chick shushed the others and told us that Freddy was in custody in the Falmouth jail, over on the mainland. I listened with astonishment as Chick said that Barry was responsible.

"Barry?" I repeated stupidly. "You?" I asked, turning to a flushed and smiling Barry.

Barry shrugged modestly, still grinning like mad.

"What happened?" Mom asked.

Chick told how Barry, after leaving our house Saturday morning, had come to derby headquarters to ask what was going on.

"Hell, you tell it, Barry," said Chick. "You're the hero here."

"Well," said Barry, "Otis told me the whole story,

and I got to thinking about how Freddy had said he wanted to mount the fish and his buddy had told him to get rid of it. And it seemed to me that maybe Freddy wouldn't listen to him. From what I'd heard, Freddy was the kind of guy who would want that fish around so he could show off a little bit. But he couldn't go to a taxidermist here on the island because he'd get caught. So I started calling taxidermists on the mainland and asking if anyone had brought in a big striped bass. On my third call, bingo! Freddy didn't go too far away, just right over on the ferry to Falmouth. Anyway, I called the folks here at headquarters and they called the police."

"Tell them about the mercury," said Chick. Turning to me, he added, "This is incredible."

Barry went on. "I told the taxidermist there might be mercury in the fish somewhere, and he laughed. He knew the trick. Apparently, all you have to do is slide a tube into the fish's flesh, pour liquid mercury into the tube, remove the tube, and there you have it: a fish with added weight that is almost impossible to detect unless you fillet the fish and cut up the meat."

Everyone murmured with astonishment.

"Now we've got all the evidence we need," said the police chief. "Poor Freddy. He got into something way over his head. He never was too smart, and he sure wasn't the brains behind this operation. He says the other guy, whose name is Roy Barrow, by the way, saw him catch the big fish six days before the contest. It was Barrow's idea to keep it alive, add the mercury, and split the prize money when they won."

"What about the big guy—Roy Barrow?" I asked. "Did you catch him yet?"

"No, but we will," said the chief. "Make no mistake about that."

"What will happen to them?" I asked.

"They'll be brought up on charges of grand larceny, Ben, and that's serious business."

I watched dumbly as Mom and Barry talked. I could hardly believe it—Barry Lester playing detective and saving the day. I had a sudden thought. "Barry," I asked, "were you down at the docks Saturday night, looking for Freddy?"

"Yes," said Barry. "I thought I might find him and talk some sense into him. That was before I had the idea about calling the taxidermists. I didn't find him, of course, because he was over in Falmouth."

I shook my head admiringly. I couldn't help it. Who would have figured Barry for a hero? It wasn't hard to see why he'd done it. He was looking at my mom like a dog waiting to be scratched. And Mom was looking back at him with the kind of smile I hadn't seen in a long time.

Just then the microphone gave a piercing screech. Everyone looked up at Otis Pritchard, who began welcoming us all to the Forty-seventh Annual Martha's

Vineyard Striped Bass Derby. Several people made speeches and everyone pretended to listen, but we were all waiting for the big announcement. Because of the last-minute discovery about Freddy's fish, no one knew for sure who had won the contest, and you could just feel the suspense in the room.

The police chief made some grave comments on the seriousness of cheating in an event such as the derby, and said how sad he was that such a thing had happened on our island. He said he hoped nothing like it would ever happen again, and everyone cheered.

Finally the winners were announced. The small prizes were awarded first, and we all clapped and whistled as the names were read. I whooped and hollered when it was announced that Jeff's mother had won second place with her big bluefish. Everyone knew Gus Rogers, and no one was surprised to hear that he was the big winner, with an eighteen-and-three-quarter-pound blue caught off the shore at Wasque.

The award ceremony ended with Chick saying solemnly that no stripers had been entered, not legally, anyway. "But that doesn't mean they aren't out there," he said. "Someday, if we're careful, these waters will be filled once again with striped bass. And maybe someday someone really will break Jack Daggett's record."

Mom caught my eye and smiled.

"But for now," Chick finished, "it stands."

Everyone cheered.

After we had congratulated Mrs. Manning and tcased her about what she was going to do with all her money, we were ready to go.

"Ben," said Barry, "I was wondering if you and your mother would like to go out for ice cream before you head home."

I was scratching some itchy, red bumps on my legs. Sure enough, I *had* gotten poison ivy, just like a silly tourist.

I looked up at Mom, then at Barry's eager face. "Okay," I said. "Sounds good to me."